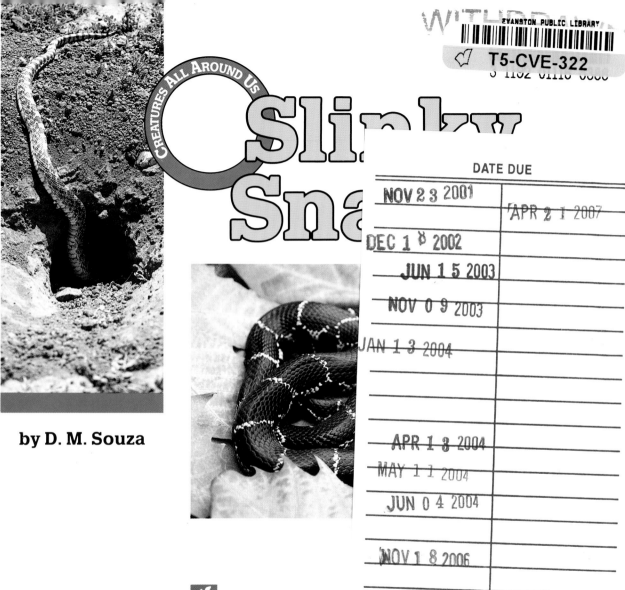

CREATURES ALL AROUND US

Slinky
Sna

by D. M. Souza

Carolrhoda L

Library of Congress Cataloging-in-Publication Data

Souza, D. M. (Dorothy M.)
  Slinky snakes / by D.M. Souza.
    p.   cm. — (Creatures all around us)
  Includes index.
  Summary: Describes the physical characteristics, habits, habitats, and life cycle of various kinds of snakes.
  ISBN 0-87614-711-2
  1. Snakes—Juvenile literature. [1. Snakes.] I. Title.
II. Series: Souza, D. M. (Dorothy M.). Creatures all around us.
QL666.O6S68 1992
597.96—dc20   91-32436
                                   CIP
                                    AC

Manufactured in the United States of America

1 2 3 4 5 6 7 8 9 10 01 00 99 98 97 96 95 94 93 92

Snakes live in almost every part of the world.

Slinky Snakes

It has no ears and its eyes never close. Its scaly body moves noiselessly and slips easily out of sight. It is called a "snake," a word that can mean sneak.

Like lizards, turtles, crocodiles, and alligators, snakes belong to a group of animals known as reptiles. All have skin that feels like leather and body temperatures that change with the temperature around them.

Snakes and other cold-blooded, or **ectothermic** (ek-tuh-THUR-mik), animals have a hard time keeping warm. They depend on the sun. But even on hot summer days, their body temperatures are only 80 or 85 degrees. Normally your temperature stays at about 98.6 no matter what the air temperature is.

Snakes like to be warm, but not too warm. If the weather is hot, they look for shady places to hide during the day. If they cannot escape the heat, they may die in less than half an hour.

Like you and me, snakes have **vertebrae** (VURT-uh-bray). These are short sections of backbones connected to one another by movable joints. People have 24 vertebrae, but some American snakes have several hundred. They also have pairs of ribs attached to each vertebra. All of these bones and joints make it possible for snakes to twist and turn in every direction.

A western ribbon snake warms itself in the sun.

Snakes can twist and turn their bodies with ease.

Two main layers of skin cover the reptile's body. The inner layer, or **dermis** (DUR-mis), is soft and stretchy. The outer layer, or **epidermis** (ep-uh-DUR-mis), is made of scaly material called **keratin** (KER-uh-tin). Keratin is also found in our fingernails and toenails and is tough and waterproof.

You can see the ridges that run down the middle of this cottonmouth's keeled scales.

Snakes' scales can be large or small, round, square, oval, or many-sided. They can be **keeled**, with ridges down the middle, or smooth. Some snakes have scales that overlap like shingles on a roof. On others, they fit tightly together like pieces of a jigsaw puzzle. There may be more than 100 rows of scales on one type of snake and as few as 10 on another. All scales serve as armor to protect the reptiles' bodies.

A snake never blinks or closes its eyes. It has no movable eyelids. Instead, a clear film, or **spectacle** (SPEK-tuh-kuhl), covers its eyes and keeps out dirt and flying dust.

Each time a snake flicks its forked tongue in and out of its mouth, it is "smelling" the air. Tiny specks of dust catch on the tips of the tongue. The snake puts the tips into its **Jacobson's organ**, two small holes near the roof of its mouth. The snake uses the Jacobson's organ to examine the dust and determine if food is nearby.

Snakes' eyes are not protected by eyelids.

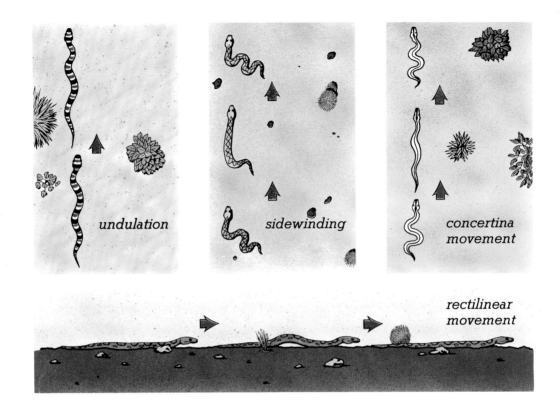

undulation

sidewinding

concertina movement

rectilinear movement

If you have ever watched a snake move across the ground or up a tree, you may have wondered how it could crawl or climb without arms or legs. It uses powerful muscles and a row of widened scales on its undersides to push against any object it can find. Without such things as rocks, grass, clumps of dirt, or bark, the snake would not be able to move.

8

Different snakes travel in different ways, and many have more than one way of moving. Some snakes can grip the ground in several places and move by pushing back and forth against the ground. They move like caterpillars, and the tracks they leave behind are straight. Snakes that travel in this way are said to use rectilinear (rek-tuh-LIHN-ee-uhr) movement.

Many snakes, including racers and king snakes, move by wriggling from side to side. They trace a series of S's over the ground. This is known as undulation (un-juh-LAY-shun) or serpentine (SUHR-pen-teen) movement.

This cottonmouth is moving by undulation, or serpentine movement.

On smooth ground, some snakes throw their heads and necks forward. Scales under their necks grip the earth. Then the snakes pull the rest of their bodies forward. They loop them back and forth in folds like those in an accordion or concertina. This is why their movement is called concertina movement.

Some snakes that live in sandy areas have a special method of traveling known as sidewinding. They lift their head and the front part of their bodies off the ground and throw them forward. The rest of their bodies roll sideways in S-shaped waves. Whenever they move, they appear to be looking over their "shoulders."

All snakes can swim, but some, such as water snakes, spend more time than others in ponds, lakes, or streams. If frightened, they will dive underwater and hide between rocks on the bottom. At other times they may sun themselves on the banks or rest under logs or piles of leaves.

Snakes have been around since the days of dinosaurs. There are nearly 3,000 different species (SPEE-sheez), or kinds, of snakes living around the world today. They can be found in deserts, forests, meadows, lakes, ponds, and even oceans. About 117 species live in the United States and Canada. While a few are dangerous, all are among the most fascinating creatures living around us.

Right: *A boa constrictor uses concertina movement to climb a tree trunk.*
Below: *A water snake sits on a water lily in a pond.*

Alive

A female rough green snake curls around her week-old eggs.

Hidden under a clump of decaying leaves on the forest floor are five white, leathery-looking eggs. As the August sun peeks through the trees and warms the spot, something begins to happen. One of the eggs rocks back and forth. After a while, a small hole appears in the shell. Slowly it grows longer and wider. Almost two hours later, a young rough green snake wriggles out of its egg case.

The snakelet's gray-green body is about 16 inches long. Fastened to its upper jaw is a triangular tooth that it has used to tear its way out of the tough shell. In a day or two, this egg tooth will drop off.

12

A black cricket leaps across a clearing and lands nearby. The newborn snake does not hear it because it has no ears. It feels the vibrations of the cricket's movements down the length of its body. Even though the little snake spots the cricket, it does not try to catch it. Weeks may pass before it will be hungry enough to eat.

Several other eggs have begun rocking back and forth, but the young green snake pays no attention to them. Instead it slithers away. It will probably never see its relatives now breaking out of their shells.

A rough green snake hatches from its egg.

A female bull snake lays her eggs in the sand.

A little more than half of the known snakes in the world are hatched from eggs. Each spring, females lay from two to one hundred leathery white or pale yellow eggs. They hide them in abandoned gopher holes, in decaying logs, or under piles of leaves and sand. Most do not stay to guard the eggs. Snakes that give birth in this way are said to be **oviparous** (oh-VIP-uh-ruhs).

14

Other snakes, such as water snakes and garter snakes, do not hatch from eggs. They develop inside their mothers' bodies in a cellophane-like covering called a **chorion** (KOR-ee-ahn). At birth or soon afterward, the covering breaks, and the young slip out. Snakes that bear young in this way are called **viviparous** (vih-VIP-uh-ruhs).

Soon after birth, all snakes go their own way. They must be especially careful when they move around. Mammals, birds, fish, and even other reptiles try to catch and eat them. Sometimes people kill them out of fear or ignorance. This is why snakelets spend most of their time in hiding.

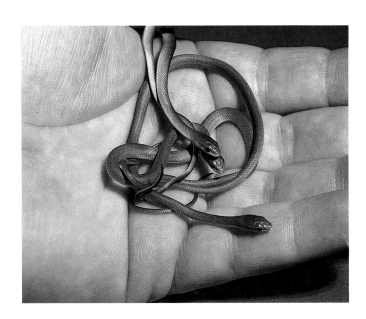

Three newborn rough green snakes huddle together in a human hand.

New Skin

The milky film over this bull snake's eyes is a sign that it is about to molt.

Resting beside a rocky stream is a young garter snake. Its skin is dull-looking and hangs loosely around its body.

For almost a week, the snake has been hiding in an abandoned burrow near the edge of a stream. Its eyes have been covered with a milky film that has made it almost blind. Today, however, the film has disappeared, and the snake begins to move slowly out of its burrow.

It touches the ground with its tongue several times, then pushes its body forward as if searching for something. It finds a rough log and immediately rubs its face against it. Again and again it does this until the skin on its entire face is pushed back around its neck. Wriggling and squirming, the snake slowly peels off its old epidermis, the way you might pull off a sock. The snake leaves its epidermis inside out on the ground. Then the reptile crawls a short distance away in a bright new skin. Its body looks wet and slimy, though it is actually smooth and dry.

A young racer rubs against the ground to remove its old skin.

A cloudy liquid oozes from a snake's epidermis shortly before it molts.

All snakes **molt**, or shed their skins, in this way. It takes from 10 minutes to an hour or longer for the snake to slip out of its skin. Big snakes take longer than little ones.

The first sign that a snake is ready to molt is the appearance of the milky film over its eyes. Next, a liquid oozes from its dermis. This loosens the epidermis and makes it dull-looking.

18

A speckled king snake left this skin behind after molting.

After about a week, the reptile's eyes clear and the fluid under its skin dries. The creature begins looking for some rough object to rub against.

Young snakes molt very soon after they are born or hatched. Small snakes grow quickly and molt more often than larger ones. Older snakes change skins only once or twice each year.

Big Mouth

Snakes use their tongues to help find out if their prey is nearby.

A gray rat munches on weed seeds at the edge of a meadow. Nearby, the smooth, dark body of a racer noiselessly slips over the earth with its head held high. The snake flicks out its tongue several times and catches the scent of food.

Suddenly it jumps forward with lightning speed and grabs the rat's head between its teeth. The animal struggles to escape. But with part of its body the racer presses its victim, or **prey**, against the ground until it stops squirming. Then it begins to swallow the creature alive.

20

A corn snake grips a field mouse in its jaws.

Although most snakes have sharp, inward-curving teeth, they do not use them for biting or chewing. Instead, they use them for gripping victims and moving them down their throats.

A snake's mouth can open very wide. It can take in a creature four or five times thicker than its own body. Several things make this possible.

The bones of the snake's head are very loosely joined together. Upper and lower jaws are each divided into two parts, and each part moves by itself.

When the racer begins its meal, the teeth on one side of its jaws hold the rat's head. Those on the other side move forward over the head. The action switches from side to side, and it looks as if the snake's jaws and teeth are "walking" over the rat's body.

Large amounts of saliva help move the rat along and begin the work of digesting the meal. After the rat moves past the snake's mouth, powerful muscles squeeze it farther down the reptile's body. As the rat moves along, the snake's ribs stretch out to make room for it.

Snakes that eat insects, earthworms, salamanders, fish, or lizards take only a few seconds to gulp their food. But snakes that capture larger animals, such as rabbits or pigs, take hours to finish a meal.

Many snakes swallow their victims alive. Others, such as king snakes, bull snakes, and boas, first wrap their bodies around their prey until they stop breathing. Then they swallow them. These snakes are called constrictors (kuhn-STRIK-tuhrz).

Snakes do not eat every day but may feast once a week or only once a month. Some can go without food for a year. When they do have a meal, it is a big one—enough to last them for a long time. If you had as big a meal as a snake's, you would probably have to eat 14 or 15 hamburgers. And unlike the snake, you would soon be hungry again.

Above: *You can see the mouse that this copperhead has just eaten moving down through its body.* Below: *Constrictors, such as this boa, kill their prey before eating them.*

Venom

Pit vipers, such as this timber rattlesnake, have pits between their eyes and nostrils.

As the sun sets and a slight breeze cools the land, night creatures begin stirring. A young rattlesnake crawls out from under a rocky ledge. It has not eaten in several weeks and is hungry.

The snake's forked tongue slips in and out of its triangular-shaped head. Between its eyes and nostrils are two deep hollows, or pits. These pits are organs that sense the heat coming from the body of another animal. They help the snake find and strike a victim even in the dark.

24

Rattlesnakes have bony rings, or rattles, at the tips of their tails.

Rattlers and other poisonous snakes such as cottonmouths and copperheads all have these hollows in their heads. Such snakes are known as pit vipers.

A falling branch startles the rattler. It coils its body and makes a buzzing noise by vibrating the bony rings on the end of its tail. It does this when frightened or threatened. There are five rings on the snake's tail now. Another will appear when the snake molts again.

After a few minutes, the rattler continues its hunt. With tongue poking in and out, it follows the scent of an animal into a nearby thicket.

Suddenly it spots a jackrabbit and leaps forward almost half the length of its body. It sinks two long fangs into the creature's neck and floods the wound with **venom** (VEH-nuhm), or poison.

The venom of all poisonous snakes is really a special kind of saliva. It is clear, slightly yellowish, and deadly. It helps the snake kill prey quickly. In minutes small animals stop breathing and can be swallowed without a struggle.

Venom is stored in glands on either side of the snake's head. During a strike, powerful muscles squeeze the poison through two fangs and into the victim.

A scientist squeezes venom from a rattlesnake's fangs. Rattlesnake venom is highly poisonous.

This cottonmouth is unfolding its fangs as a warning. If it continues to feel threatened, it will strike.

When not in use, the fangs of the rattler are folded inward against the roof of its mouth. As the mouth opens, they spring forward. Once in a while, they sink so deeply into prey that they cannot be pulled out, and the snake has to leave its fangs behind. New ones grow to replace them in a few weeks.

Some poisonous snakes such as copperheads and cotton-mouths have fangs similar to those of rattlers. Others such as coral snakes have shorter ones and do not fold them in their mouths. The tips rest in pockets outside each lower jaw.

Copperheads and other poisonous snakes use their venom to kill prey quickly.

After about five minutes, the rattler grabs the lifeless creature by the head and begins swallowing it. It will take the snake an hour or longer to finish this meal. Then it will find a hiding place where it can rest while the weight in its stomach is digested.

On Guard

Hognose snakes puff up their bodies and hiss to warn away intruders.

A gray-and-white cat is searching for mice in a field of tall grass. Also moving in the grass is a large hognose snake with an upturned snout.

The cat is busy sniffing the ground and does not see the snake now staring at it. As the cat creeps closer, the reptile spreads its long ribs and flattens out its head and neck. They become almost twice as wide as normal. The hognose takes a deep breath and its body swells. Then it lets out a loud hiss and shakes its tail.

This hognose snake is playing dead.

The hair on the cat's neck stands up straight. As the snake presses its body against the ground, the cat also crouches low. It slowly creeps forward, sniffing the ground as it moves. All at once the snake opens its mouth and rolls over on its back as if dead.

The cat pokes one paw at the strange-looking creature, trying to make it move. When nothing happens, it turns and goes back to hunting mice. After a few minutes, the hognose raises its head and looks around. Seeing that the cat is gone, it flips over on its belly and slips away.

Most snakes, like the hognose, have clever ways of escaping **predators** (PREH-duh-turz), or animals that threaten them. Many use **camouflage** (KAM-uh-flahzh)—protective coloring—to help them blend into their surroundings. Copperheads, for example, look like fallen leaves and usually hide in a pile of them. Green snakes live in trees and shrubs and are hard to spot in their green hideouts.

Green snakes can easily blend in with leaves.

Other snakes use their colors to frighten enemies. When threatened, the ringneck snake curls its tail and flashes the brilliant red coloring of its underside. Most of the time predators retreat when they spot this color or the red, yellow, and black bands of the poisonous coral snake.

A number of harmless snakes, including the scarlet king snake and the banded sand snake, have similar red, yellow, and black markings. They are frequently mistaken for coral snakes. Because of this, predators leave them alone.

Some snakes, like the hognose and the pine snake, make hissing noises. Others shake their tails in dry grass or leaves. But only the rattlesnake has a tail that really "rattles."

Boas roll up into a ball when they are threatened. Garter snakes, water snakes, and king snakes give off foul odors from glands near their tails.

It's easy to see how predators can confuse the deadly coral snake (above) with the harmless scarlet king snake (below).

*A broad-winged hawk
swallows a snake.*

Snakes have many defenses because they have many enemies. Skunks, foxes, raccoon, and opossums hunt them. So too do alligators, crocodiles, hawks, and roadrunners. Deer and other animals with hooves crush them. Some snakes, such as king snakes, even eat one another. They are said to be **cannibals**.

People are perhaps the greatest enemies of snakes. Hunters take them for sport or for their skins. Others kill them because they think all snakes are dangerous. Each year millions are destroyed by cars on roads or highways.

With all these enemies, it is surprising there are so many snakes still around.

34

Hideaways

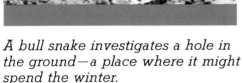

A bull snake investigates a hole in the ground—a place where it might spend the winter.

When autumn arrives and days turn cool, snakes have a difficult time. They must spend as many hours as possible in the sun. They avoid damp places and begin looking for dens or shelters in which to **hibernate**, or spend the winter.

Caves, rocky cliffs, or underground tunnels protect them from frost and cold. Many snakes return to the same dens each year. Sometimes as many as 250 snakes will huddle together for warmth.

When a snake's temperature drops to 50 degrees, its body becomes stiff and is hardly able to move. Before this happens, the reptile crawls into a sheltered place and falls into a trance. Its heartbeat slows, as do its breathing and growth rate. It is barely alive. Yet even though it does not eat for months, it loses very little weight.

Only when the sun warms the earth again do snakes crawl out of hiding. They warm their bodies in the sun and within a short time begin again their fascinating activities.

Although snakes spend most of their lives alone, they often hibernate in groups to stay warm.

Scientists who study animals group them together according to their similarities and differences. Animals that have certain features in common are placed in the same group. Snakes belong to the order, or group, of reptiles known as Squamata, and so do lizards. Within the order, there are many different families. Below are some of the members of the four families of snakes that live in the United States, along with a few facts about them.

FAMILY	EXAMPLES	SIZE IN INCHES	FAVORITE FOODS	WHERE FOUND IN THE U.S.
Boidae	rosy boas	24-42	birds, small mammals	Arizona and California
Colubridae	garter snakes	14-44	frogs, toads, worms, fish	most states
	hognose snakes	16-45	toads, lizards, fish, birds	most areas except West Coast
	bull snakes	60-84	gophers, squirrels	many areas
Viperidae (poisonous)	copperheads	30-50	birds, rodents, frogs, lizards	eastern and south central states
	rattlesnakes	15-96	birds, reptiles, small mammals	most states
Elapidae (poisonous)	Arizona coral snake	15-21	reptiles	Arizona and New Mexico

Glossary

camouflage: an animal's way of disguising itself by blending into its surroundings

cannibals: animals that eat their own kind

chorion: a covering that surrounds a developing animal inside its mother's body

dermis: the inner layer of an animal's skin

ectothermic: having a body temperature that changes depending on the temperature of the environment

epidermis: the outer layer of an animal's skin

hibernate: to spend the winter in a sleeplike state

Jacobson's organ: an organ that certain animals have that helps them smell and taste

keeled: covered with ridges

keratin: a material that makes up a reptile's outer layer of skin

molt: to shed skin

oviparous: giving birth by laying eggs

predators: animals that hunt and eat other animals

prey: animals that are killed and eaten by other animals

spectacle: a thin film that covers a snake's eyes

venom: poison that is produced in the body of an animal

vertebrae: short sections of backbone that are connected to each other

viviparous: giving birth to live young

Index